Francis Orray Ticknor

The Poems of Frank Orray Ticknor, M.D.

Francis Orray Ticknor

The Poems of Frank Orray Ticknor, M.D.

ISBN/EAN: 9783337407230

Printed in Europe, USA, Canada, Australia, Japan

Cover: Foto ©Andreas Hilbeck / pixelio.de

More available books at **www.hansebooks.com**

OF

FRANK O. TICKNOR, M.D.

EDITED BY

K. M. R.

WITH AN INTRODUCTORY NOTICE OF THE AUTHOR

BY

PAUL H. HAYNE.

———

PHILADELPHIA:

J. B. LIPPINCOTT & CO.

1879.

" Not less on him than thee the mysteries .
Within him and about him ever weigh.
*   *   *   *   *

But on the surface of his song these lie
As shadows, not as darkness; and alway
There is a human purpose in the lay."
TIMROD.

3

CONTENTS.

1*

MEMORIAL AND RELIGIOUS POEMS.

INTRODUCTORY NOTICE.

In the month of December, 1874, died, near Columbus, Georgia, one of the truest and sweetest lyric poets this country has yet produced. Nevertheless, he lived the fifty-two years of his allotted existence in comparative obscurity, and passed to the "great beyond" unknown, despite the rare originality of his genius and works, except, indeed, to that small portion of the Southern public who condescend now and then to pass from politics to poetry.

Dr. Frank O. Ticknor, born in Baldwin County, Georgia, combined in his mental and moral constitution many of the best qualities of the North and South. His father was a "New Jerseyman," a physician of great energy, while his grandparents were natives of Norwich, Connecticut. Dr. Ticknor, the elder, married into a distinguished family of Savannah, and settled for a time in that city. He died a young man, leaving his widow with three small children to support. At once she removed to the town of Columbus, exerting herself with such judicious perseverance that she succeeded in giving to her sons excellent and liberal educations.

Frank, when old enough, studied medicine in New York and Philadelphia, and soon after his graduation married Miss Rosalie Nelson, daughter of Major T.

M. Nelson, a distinguished soldier of the War of 1812, and subsequently a prominent member of Congress. A few years after this union, Dr. Ticknor purchased a farm not far from Columbus, situated on the summit of a high hill, and celebrated by tradition as the scene of a desperate Indian battle which had been *fought by torch-light*. In consequence he named this place "Torch Hill."

Anything more picturesque than the view therefrom it would be hard to imagine. The house overlooks for miles on miles the Chattahoochee Valley, full of waving grain-fields and opulent orchards.

With the poet's love of all that is pure, sweet, and natural, he soon surrounded his home with flowers and fruits. In the spring and summer I have heard it described as a perfect Eden of roses; while towards autumn the crimson foliage and blushing tints of the great mellow apples, especially if touched by sunset lights, caused the "Hill" to gleam and glitter as with the colors of fairy-land. Here in this peaceful nest Ticknor lived for nearly a quarter of a century, exceptionally blessed in his domestic relations, though more than once that Dark Presence no mortal can shun entered his household, to leave it for a season desolate. Here he dreamed high dreams and beheld pleasant visions. Art opened to his soul not one alone, but several of her fairest domains. He was a gifted musician, playing exquisitely upon the flute, and a draughtsman of the readiest skill and taste. Still I picture him always as pre-eminently the poet,—the poet "born," yet with every natural endowment purified and strengthened by careful, scholarly culture.

Thus much for one side of his life. There was

another side, stirring, practical, and often rife, as a physician's career necessarily must be, with sad or terrible details. If a spiritual "Lotos-Eater" while "sporting with his muse in the shade," he was all energy, eagerness, and well-directed power in the paths of his profession. No more experienced doctor or successful scientist than he could be found in the county which chanced to be the scene of his labors. He united a broad humanity and a tender graciousness of tone and bearing to the information of the savant and the skill of the medical expert. Everybody loved him, especially the suffering poor, to whom he devoted a great deal of his time and attention. Unostentatious, but profoundly sincere in his Christian belief and practice, he regarded the poverty-smitten and the unfortunate as pensioners directly assigned to his care by Providence.

Far and wide, among the "sand-barrens" or in the farmhouses of the neighboring valley, the good and wise physician was known and welcomed. His gleeful smile, his spontaneous criticisms (for his mind actually bubbled over with innocent humors), cheered up many a despondent invalid, and it is possible scared Despair, if not Death himself, away from the bedsides of patients just about finally to succumb.

What wonder, therefore, that when—partly through fatigue, exposure, and the unremitting discharge of duty—their benefactor was, in his turn, stricken down, to die after a brief, painful illness, the community mourned him as only those are mourned who could truly say, like Abou ben Adhem, in his vision of the Angel and the Book of Gold, "Write me as one who loved his fellow-men"?

This imperfect outline of Ticknor's life was necessary
to the full comprehension of his poetry.   " Brief swal-
low-flights of song" only were possible to a man whose
days and nights were so occupied by important and
exacting toils.   And in some respects this was fortunate,
since the comparatively little leisure enjoyed by the
poet forced him to concentrate his powers,—to utilize
them to the very best advantage.

When the great Civil War began, Ticknor had just
reached the verge of middle age.   His intellectual
forces were in their fullest bloom ; and so it is not
surprising that many of his ablest songs belong to this
period.

Look, for example, at his " Virginians of the Valley."   It is so short that we can readily quote it entire :

"THE VIRGINIANS OF THE VALLEY.

" The knightliest of the knightly race
        That, since the days of old,
    Have kept the lamp of chivalry
        Alight in hearts of gold ;
    The kindliest of the kindly band
        That, rarely hating ease,
    Yet rode with Spotswood round the land,
        And Raleigh round the seas ;

" Who climbed the blue Virginian hills
        Against embattled foes,
    And planted there, in valleys fair,
        The lily and the rose ;
    Whose fragrance lives in many lands,
        Whose beauty stars the earth,
    And lights the hearths of happy homes
        With loveliness and worth.

" We thought they slept !—the sons who kept
   The names of noble sires,
And slumbered while the darkness crept
   Around their vigil-fires ;   .
But, aye, the ' Golden Horseshoe' knights
   Their old Dominion keep,
Whose foes have found enchanted ground,
   But not a knight asleep !"

Is not this, reader, a splendid lyric? Whether you
are of the South or the North, especially now that the
old sectional animosities seem to be dying out, I feel
sure you must alike admire it. The *verve* and fire of
the conception and the simple straightforward powers
of the execution make it a most impressive ballad.
James Russell Lowell, in a recent "Ode," has elo-
quently praised Virginia ; but there is a heart-drawn
pathos, a half-subdued passion in Ticknor's poem which
seems to me more effective still. Apropos of the lat-
ter's style, James Maurice Thompson, himself so true
a lyrist, has remarked that " it is best suited to forceful
ballads. Something in the direct, clear, ringing expression of his ' Virginians' reminds us of

" ' *Mais quand la pauvre champagne*
   Fut en proie aux étrangers,
   Lui, bravant tous les dangers,
   Semblait seul tenir la campagne.'

With Ticknor, as with Béranger, strength is simplicity,
art is naturalness." Mr. Thompson continues : " Few
poets acknowledge that, to stir the feelings and reach
the inmost heart of the masses, one must make use of
those materials which are suited to the vulgar under-
standing. See the final stanza of that inimitable ballad,
' *La Vache Perdue*,' by Casimir Delavigne :

2

" ' *Un soir, à ma fenêtre,*
    Neva, pour t'abriter,
    De ta corne peut-être
    Tu reviendras heurter.
    Si la famille est morte,
        Neva,
    Qui t'ouvrira la porte ?
        Ah ! ah ! Neva !"

Now Ticknor's ballad of ' Little Giffen' is a ballad
precisely of the style of Delavigne. The opening
stanza is a bold swell of music, something clarion-
like.

" 'Out of the focal and foremost fire,
    Out of the hospital walls as dire ;
    Smitten of grape-shot and gangrene,
    (Eighteenth battle, and *he* sixteen !)
    Spectre ! such as you seldom see,
    Little Giffen, of Tennessee !'

The identical rhyme of the last couplet one loses sight
of in the exceeding terseness of the language, the out-
right vigor of the rhetorical stroke. Most poets dally
with their conceptions. But this one seizes his idea at
once, thrusts it into a position of strong relief, fastens
it there, and is done. Technically speaking, his style
is dynamic.

" Here is another verse of ' Little Giffen' :

" ' Word of gloom from the war, one day ;
    Johnson pressed at the front, they say.
    Little Giffen was up and away ;
    A tear—his first—as he bade good-by,
    Dimmed the glint of his steel-blue eye ;
    " *I'll write*, if spared." There was news of the fight ;
    But none of Giffen.—He did not write.'

The poem rounds off half-solemnly, half-playfully, thus:

> " 'I sometimes fancy that, were I king
>   Of the princely Knights of the Golden Ring,
>   With the song of the minstrel in mine ear,
>   And the tender legend that trembles here,
>   I'd give the best on his bended knee,
>   The whitest soul of my chivalry,
>   For " Little Giffen," of Tennessee.'

"Now, here is no straining after effect, *no floundering to get up a foam;* but that sturdy art which is the spirit of a genuine popular ballad."

Another poem, which explains itself,—an absolutely perfect ballad (*me judice*),—I cannot resist the pleasure of extracting. Was ever the historical incident it commemorates more feelingly and vividly described? These verses are simply entitled

" LOYAL.

> " The good Lord Douglas—dead of old—
>   In his last journeying
>   Wore at his heart, encased in gold,
>   The heart of Bruce, his king,
>
> " Through Paynim lands to Palestine—
>   For so his troth was plight—
>   To lay that gold on Christ his shrine,
>   Let fall what peril might.
>
> " By night and day, a weary way
>   Of vigil and of fight,
>   Where never rescue came by day,
>   Nor ever rest by night.

" And one by one the valiant spears
    Were smitten from his side :
And one by one the bitter tears
    Fell for the brave that died.

" Till fierce and black around his track
    He saw the combat close,
And counted but the single sword
    Against uncounted foes.

" He drew the casket from his breast,
    He bared his solemn brow !
Oh, foremost of the kingliest !
    Go ' first in battle' now !

" Where leads my Lord of Bruce, the sword
    Of Douglas shall not stay !
Forward !   We meet at Christ His feet
    In Paradise, to-day !

" The casket flashed; the battle clashed,
    Thundered, and rolled away;
And dead above the heart of Bruce
    The heart of Douglas lay !

" Loyal !   Methinks the antique mould
    Is lost, or theirs alone
Who sheltered Freedom's heart of gold,
    Like Douglas, with their own !' "

A single other lyric associated with the war and its
sorrows, and I shall close :

" UNKNOWN !

" The prints of feet are worn away,
    No more the mourners come ;
The voice of wail is mute to-day
    As his whose life is dumb.

" The world is bright with other bloom;
  Shall the sweet summer shed
Its living radiance o'er the tomb
  That shrouds the doubly dead?

" Unknown!   Beneath our Father's face
  The starlit hillocks lie;
Another rosebud! lest His grace
  Forget us when we die!"

Ah! how many thousands must be still living to whom this ballad, rounded and limpid as a tear, though simple almost to baldness in expression, must appeal with a pathos not to be resisted!

Burns himself was not more direct, more transparently honest in his metrical appeals than Ticknor.

There are no fantastic conceits, no far-fetched similes, no dilettanteism of any sort in his verses.

The man's soul—sturdy yet gentle, stalwart yet touched by a feminine sweetness—"informed" them always; and, if it can hardly be said of his lyrics that each was "polished as the bosom of a star," still the light irradiating them seldom failed to be light from the heaven of a true inspiration.

PAUL H. HAYNE.

MARTIAL AND CHIVALROUS LYRICS.

19

DEDICATION.

E. P. C.—A LILY OF THE VALLEY.

THY smile, sweet sister, on my lay,
  Is as the stars, I ween,
That brightens o'er this brilliant's ray,
  Which, else, no light had seen !
That kindles o'er some brooklet's way,
  Where, else, no song had been !

If aught of summer worth it brings
  In bloom or melodies,
'Tis little for the lyric wings
  Thy radiance taught to rise,
But little for a bird that sings
  So near his Paradise.

By Hope in many a broken home,
  And by the tears that shed
The proudest splendor of the tomb
  Above the humblest head,
This song but asks thy soul's perfume
  To crown our Quick and Dead.

THE VIRGINIANS OF THE VALLEY.

(W. N. N.)

THE knightliest of the knightly race .
    That, since the days of old,
Have kept the lamp of chivalry
    Alight in hearts of gold ;
The kindliest of the kindly band .
    That, rarely hating ease,
Yet rode with Spotswood round the land,
    And Raleigh round the seas ;

Who climbed the blue Virginian hills
    Against embattled foes,
And planted there, in valleys fair,
    The lily and the rose ;
Whose fragrance lives in many lands,
    Whose beauty stars the earth,
And lights the hearths of happy homes
    With loveliness and worth.

We thought they slept !—the sons who kept
    The names of noble sires,
And slumbered while the darkness crept
    Around their vigil-fires ;
But, aye, the "Golden Horseshoe" knights
    Their old Dominion keep,
Whose foes have found enchanted ground,
    But not a knight asleep!

A BATTLE BALLAD.

TO GENERAL J. E. JOHNSTON.

A SUMMER Sunday morning,
  July the twenty-first,
In eighteen hundred sixty-one,
  The storm of battle burst.

For many a year the thunder
  Had muttered deep and low,
And many a year, through hope and fear,
  The storm had gathered slow.

Now hope had fled the hopeful,
  And fear was with the past ;
And on Manassas' cornfields
  The tempest broke at last.

A wreath above the pine-tops,
  The booming of a gun ;
A ripple on the cornfields,
  And the battle was begun.

A feint upon our centre,
  While the foeman massed his might,
For our swift and sure destruction,
  With his overwhelming "right."

All the summer air was darkened
  With the tramping of their host;
All the Sunday stillness broken
  By the clamor of their boast.

With their lips of savage shouting,
  And their eyes of sullen wrath,
Goliath, with the weaver-beam,
  The champion of Gath.

Are they men who guard the passes,
  On our "left" so far away?
In thy cornfields, O Manassas!
  Are they *men* who fought to-day?

Our *boys* are brave and gentle,
  And their brows are smooth and white;
Have they grown to *men*, Manassas,
  In the watches of a night?

Beyond the grassy hillocks
  There are tents that glimmer white;
Beneath the leafy covert
  There is steel that glistens bright.

There are eyes of watchful reapers
  Beneath the summer leaves,
With a glitter as of sickles
  Impatient for the sheaves.

They are men who guard the passes,
  They are men who bar the ford;
Stands our David at Manassas,
  The champion of the Lord.

They are men who guard our altars,
  And beware, ye sons of Gath,
The deep and deathful silence
  Of the lion in your path.

Lo ! the foe was mad for slaughter,
  And the whirlwind hurtled on ;
But our *boys* had grown to heroes,
  They were *lions*, every one.

And they stood a wall of iron,
  And they shone a wall of flame,
And they beat the baffled tempest
  To the caverns whence it came.

And Manassas' sun descended
  On their armies crushed and torn,
On a battle bravely ended,
  · On a nation grandly born.

The laurel and the cypress,
  The glory and the grave,
We pledge to thee, O Liberty !
  The life-blood of the brave.

"OUR LEFT."

(MANASSAS.)

FROM dawn to dark they stood
That long midsummer day,
While fierce and fast
The battle blast
Swept rank on rank away.

From dawn to dark they fought,
With legions torn and cleft;
And still the wide
Black battle-tide
Poured deadlier on "Our Left."

They closed each ghastly gap;
They dressed each shattered rank;
They knew—how well—
That Freedom fell
With that exhausted flank.

"Oh, for a thousand men
Like these that melt away!"
And down they came,
With steel and flame,
Four thousand to the fray!

Right through the blackest cloud
Their lightning path they cleft;

And triumph came
With deathless fame
To our unconquered " Left."

Ye, of your sons secure,
  Ye, of your dead bereft,
    Honor the brave
    Who died to save
Your all upon our " Left."

LITTLE GIFFEN.

OUT of the focal and foremost fire,
Out of the hospital walls as dire ;
Smitten of grape-shot and gangrene,
(Eighteenth battle, and *he* sixteen !)
Spectre ! such as you seldom see,
Little Giffen, of Tennessee !

"Take him and welcome !" the surgeons said ;
Little the doctor can help the dead !
So we took him ; and brought him where
The balm was sweet in the summer air ;
And we laid him down on a wholesome bed—
Utter Lazarus, heel to head !

And we watched the war with abated breath,—
Skeleton Boy against skeleton Death.
Months of torture, how many such ?
Weary weeks of the stick and crutch ;

And still a glint of the steel-blue eye
Told of a spirit that *wouldn't* die,

And didn't.   Nay, more ! in death's despite
The crippled skeleton "learned to write."
Dear mother, at first, of course ; and then
Dear captain, inquiring about the men.
Captain's answer : of eighty-and-five,
Giffen and I are left alive.

Word of gloom from the war, one day ;
Johnson pressed at the front, they say.
Little Giffen was up and away ;
A tear—his first—as he bade good-by,
Dimmed the glint of his steel-blue eye.
"*I'll write*, if spared !"   There was news of the fight ;
But none of Giffen.—He did not write.

I sometimes fancy that, were I king
Of the princely Knights of the Golden Ring,
With the song of the minstrel in mine ear,
And the tender legend that trembles here,
I'd give the best on his bended knee,
The whitest soul of my chivalry,
For "Little Giffen," of Tennessee.

THE SWORD IN THE SEA.

THE billows plunge like steeds that bear
  The knights with snow-white crests;
The sea-winds blare like bugles where
  The Alabama rests.

Old glories from their splendor-mists
  Salute with trump and hail
The sword that held the ocean lists
  Against the world in mail.

And down from England's storied hills,
  From lyric slopes of France,
The old bright wine of valor fills
  The chalice of Romance.

For here was Glory's tourney-field,
  The tilt-yard of the sea;
The battle-path of kingly wrath,
  And kinglier courtesy.

And down the deeps, in sumless heaps,
  The gold, the gem, the pearl,
In one broad blaze of splendor, belt
  Great England like an earl.

And there they rest, the princeliest
  Of earth's regalia gems,
The starlight of our Southern Cross,
  The sword of Raphael Semmes.

3*

CANNON SONG.

TO CAPTAIN E. A. DAWSON.

AHA! a song for the trumpet's tongue,
   For the bugle to sing before us,
When our gleaming guns, like clarions,
   Shall thunder in battle chorus!
Where the rifles ring, where the bullets sing,
   Where the black bombs whistle o'er us,
With rolling wheel and rattling peal
   We'll thunder in battle chorus!

CHORUS.

With the cannon's flash and the cannon's crash,
   With the cannon's roar and rattle,
Let Freedom's sons, with their shouting guns,
   Go down to their country's battle!

Their brassy throats shall learn the notes
   That make old tyrants quiver,
Till the war is won or each Tyrrell gun
   Grows cold with our hearts forever.
Where the laurel waves o'er our brothers' graves,
   Who have gone to their rest before us,
Here's a requiem shall sound for them,
   And thunder in battle chorus!
         With the cannon's flash, etc.

By the light that lies in our Southern skies,
   By the spirits that watch above us;
By the gentle hands in our summer lands,
   And the gentle hearts that love us,
Our fathers' faith let us keep till death,
   Their fame in its cloudless splendor,
As men who stand for their mother-land,
   And die—but never surrender!

With the cannon's flash, with the cannon's crash,
   With the cannon's roar and rattle,
Let Freedom's sons, with their gleaming guns,
   Go down to their country's battle!

"ORA PACE."

Ora Pace! Pray for Peace!
Till these times of tumult cease!
Ye with heavy hearts and eyes,
Watchers as the war-clouds rise,
Though the shadows still increase,
Gentle spirits! Pray for Peace!

Ora Pace! Ye that lift
The nation's weapons, keen and swift,
Ere ye loose the thunder, pray
That the wrath may pass away!
Ere the lightnings ye release,
Patriot statesmen, Pray for Peace!

Ora Pace! Ye that stand
The shield and summer of the land;
Though the blood is hot and high,
Bounding for the battle-cry,
Remember, boys, whose kiss ye bear,
And pray for peace, ye sons of Prayer!

Ora Pace! Who shall tread
Our Lilies, when that prayer is said?
Dark may be the sullen tide
Of the stranger's lust and pride,
But, our God shall still increase
The strength that strikes and prays for Peace.

———

THE RIVER.

HOLD to the giant river,
    Ye, with a giant claim!
Yours from the great All-Giver,
    Yours in Jehovah's name!
By fireside, field, and altar,
    By temple, by grove, by grave,
        By the smiles and tears
        Of a hundred years,
By the life-time toil of your pioneers
    And the life-blood of your braves.

De Soto sleeps in its bosom,
    Yet the dreamer's dream was truth,

And he left to your watch the waters
  Of the world's immortal youth ;
Yours from the fount of story,
  Yours till oblivion's wave,
By the *deed* of your day of glory,
  By the *seal* of your Sidney's grave,
For yourselves, for your sons, forever,
  And ever, to hold and to have :
The broad and abounding river,
  Down to the salt sea wave ;
    While the waters flow,
    While the grasses grow,
Till the last of your race lies cold and low,
  Or God forgets the brave !

--- ---

VIRGINIA.

TRIPLE triumph to thy spears,
        Virginia !
Daughter of the cavaliers,
        Virginia !
Let the timbrel and the dance
Tell of thine anointed lance,
Tell of thy deliverance,
        Virginia !

On the shore and by the sea,
        Virginia !
Thou hast triumphed gloriously,
        Virginia !

Loftier head of haughtier foe,
Laid in dust of battle low,
Never decked thy saddle-bow,
Virginia!

Awful through thy blinding tears,
Virginia!
Blazed the light of buried years,
Virginia!
Spirits of the mighty dead
Followed still thy battle tread,
Followed where thy falchion led,
Virginia!

Heart to heart, they smote again,
Virginia!
The savage and the Saracen,
Virginia!
Soul to soul, as son and sire,
Sword of wrath and heart of fire,
Swept to vengeance swift and dire,
Virginia!

Mailed in thine immortal wrong,
Virginia!
Let thy sorrows make thee strong,
Virginia!
Clothe thee, quarter-deck to keel,
Harness thee from head to heel,
Massive oak and sheeted steel,
Virginia!

Onward yet, thou heart of gold,
            Virginia !
First in freedom's fight of old,
            Virginia !
Forward yet ! the grace that flings
The heart to death above a king's
Shall follow where thy bugle sings,
            Virginia !

THE GAP.

(BOONSBORO' GAP, OR SOUTH MOUNTAIN PASS.)

TO D. H. HILL.

PROUDER than Persia's noontide was
The dawn that hurled yon bannered mass,
The banded Orient, on the pass
Barred by thine arm, *Leonidas !*

But prouder still the vestal lights
Of glory on these vigil heights ;
And proudest yet the hand that writes,
Here wrestled Arthur and his Knights !

LABOR—SACRIFICE.

WITH THE DEVICE OF A BULLOCK; FROM THE SEAL OF A SOUTHERN GENTLEMAN.

THAT cream was of the kindliest strain
    That meadow ever drew
From sunlight and the summer rain,
  · From darkness and the dew !
That left no stain in yonder vein
    But Heaven's—the sapphire blue.
        That gentleman, we knew,
        So gentle and so true ;
        A knight whose signet bore
        A "Bullock," and no more ;
        A quaint device, by Sacrifice
        And Labor won of yore !

And matchless sweet the golden wheat
    That met and moulded him,
A man complete from head to feet
    In grace of soul and limb ;
That lent his gaze the lion's blaze,
    His smile—who smiles like *him ?*
        Ah ! tremulous and dim,
        Through tears we think of him,
        The knight whose signet bore
        That quaint device of "Sacrifice"
        And "Labor," and no more.

Upon no statelier sight
  The circling sun hath smiled,
Nor oak of loftier height
  Dropped shade so sweet and mild ;
Where love came down like light,
  And happiness grew wild !
      The sage, the little child,
      Peasant and prince, have smiled
      Around his knees who bore
    , The Bullock ; quaint device
      Of Toil and Sacrifice,
      Which all his fathers wore,
      Which he shall wear no more.

For he is dead !   Beneath the tread
  Of battle, in the roar
That rent the sod, his face to God,
  He went, and came no more !
The fragrance of the path he trod
  In sacrifice is o'er.
      Yet all the kindliest rays
      Of all the knightliest days
      Kindled forevermore,
      Around the cross he bore ;
      Around the quaint device
      Of Toil and Sacrifice
      That our great Bishop* wore.

---

* Rt. Rev. Stephen Elliott, of Georgia.

OUR GREAT CAPTAIN.

"STONEWALL" JACKSON.

THE shout of the battle hath fled,
　　The flame of it fallen dim ;
We are sick of the war, it is said,
　　Weary of tales so grim.
But to-night, and our captain lies dead ;
　　To-night, and we think of him.

Knight of the cloudless sun,
　　Ithuriel of the spear,
Whose touch was the foe undone,
　　Whose name was a nation's cheer ;
His voice and victory's—*one*,
　　Vanished in silence here.

But the flash of. a fusillade,
　　In the gloom that hath lifted never,
And our guide and our glory fade
　　In the wilderness forever,
Till we follow his smile to the shade
　　Of the Tree, by the Eden river.

In the shadows with no release
　　From the sorrows that haunt us grim,
Where our hopes at their fountain cease,
　　And the light of the Heaven is dim,
It is strength, it is hope, it is peace,
　　It is triumph to think of *him*.

ALBERT SIDNEY JOHNSTON.

SHILOH.

His soul to God! on a battle-psalm!
  The soldier's plea to Heaven!
From the victor-wreath to the shining Palm:
From the battle's core to the central calm,
  And peace of God in Heaven.

Oh, Land! in your midnight of mistrust
  The golden gates flew wide,
And the kingly soul of your wise and just
Passed in light from the house of dust
  To the Home of the Glorified.

GRACIE, OF ALABAMA.

[TO GENERAL R. H. CHILTON.]

On, sons of mighty stature,
  And souls that match the best;—
When nations name their jewels
  Let Alabama rest.

Gracie, of Alabama !
  'Twas on that dreadful day
When howling hounds were fiercest,
  With Petersburg at bay.

Gracie, of Alabama,
  Walked down the lines with Lee,
Marking through mists of gunshot
  The clouds of enemy ;

Scanning the Anaconda
  At every scale and joint ;
And halting, glasses levelled
  At gaze on " Dead Man's Point."

Thrice, Alabama's warning
  Fell on a heedless ear,
While the relentless lead-storm,
  Converging, hurtled near ;

Till straight before his chieftain,
  Without or sound or sign,
He stood, a shield the grandest,
  Against the Union line :

And then the glass was lowered,
  And voice that faltered not
Said, in its measured cadence,
  " Why, Gracie, you'll be shot !"

And Alabama answered :
  " The South will pardon me
If the ball that goes through Gracie
  Comes short of Robert Lee !"

Swept a swift flash of crimson
　　Athwart the chieftain's cheek,
And the eyes whose glance was " knighthood"
　　Spake as no king could speak.

And side by side with Gracie
　　He turned from shot and flame ;
Side by side with Gracie
　　Up the grand aisle of Fame.

LEE.

THIS wondrous valley ! hath it spells
　　And golden alchemies,
That so its chaliced splendor dwells
　　In these imperial eyes?

This man hath breathed all balms of light,
　　And quaffed all founts of grace,
Till Glory, on the mountain height,
　　Has met him face to face.

Ye kingly hills ! ye dimpled dells !
　　Haunt of the eagle—dove,
Grant us your wine of woven spells
　　To grow like him we love !

4*

"UNKNOWN."

THE prints of feet are worn away,
  No more the mourners come ;
The voice of wail is mute to-day
  As his whose life is dumb.

The world is bright with other bloom ;
  Shall the sweet summer shed
Its living radiance o'er the tomb
  That shrouds the doubly dead ?

Unknown !   Beneath our Father's face
  The star-lit hillocks lie ;
Another rosebud ! lest His grace
  Forget us when we die.

THE GRAYS AT HOME.

UP the hill, mine honored Gray !
We are going home—" To stay !"

Around the hill, below the heights,
Cling the glooms and gleam the lights.

Glamour of the evil eyes !
Spume of hate that never dies !

Let the cauldron boil below !
Wish the world a fairer foe !

Balsam to our battle-scars
Climbing nearer to the stars.

Homeward with the rapture that
Beached the ark on Ararat.

All the ways of war and weather
We have worn the harness leather.

Days with never cymbal-beat,
Save the music of thy feet.

Nights with never star or guide,
Save the glimmer of thy hide.

Stained with all the tints of toil
And "variations of the soil,"

Deeper tinct with every stain
The tireless wine-press wrings from pain,

Not the frosted hills display
Richer dapple, oh, my Gray !

Not the vales at vintage hold
Riper deeps of gloom and gold.

Up the hill, oh, grace and speed,
And power unplummeted of need !

These have cheered the night agone,
These are musical at dawn.

Ringing to the bright'ning dome,
Climbing upwards, onwards, *home !*

Far above the cauldron's spume,
With starry cross and stainless plume,

We have shared the " corn" and heather,
We are going *home* together.

On thy crest this loving sign,
Be my Lord's white mark on mine !

GRAY.

SOMETHING so human-hearted
   In a tint that ever lies
Where a splendor has just departed
   And a glory is yet to rise !

Gray in the solemn gloaming,
   Gray in the dawning skies ;
In the old man's crown of honor,
   In the little maiden's eyes.

Gray mists o'er the meadows brooding,
   Whence the world must draw its best ;
Gray gleams in the churchyard shadows,
   Where all the world would " rest."

Gray gloom in the grand cathedral,
  Where the " Glorias" are poured,
And, with angel and archangel,
  We wait the coming Lord.

Silvery gray for the bridal,
  Leaden gray for the pall;
For urn, for wreath, for life and death,
  Ever the *Gray* for all.

Gray in the very sadness
  Of ashes and sackcloth; yea,
While our raiment of beauty and gladness
  Tarries, our *tears* shall stay;
And our souls shall smile through their sadness,
  And our hearts shall wear the *Gray*.

HOLLAND.

BRAVE Holland ! of the broad sea nursed,
Where the blue billows roll and burst
From the bleak, bitter north. In thee,
Star-crowned with peace and liberty,
We hail " the Venus of the Sea !"

The heart and home of wealth and worth,
The Eden glory of the earth;
A sea of billowy verdure drest
In rippling green, with lily crest.
In all our woes across the sea,
Bright Holland, Georgia cries to thee !

Scourged by a more than bitter tide,
With the black billows howling wide ;
Wrecked to her naked soil and sky,
Reft of her *all* but memory !
Dear sister of like sorrows, we
Turn in our wasting woes to thee !

Of old, thy virgin liberty
Returned, a vestal, to the sea !
And *ours ?* Her bleeding feet impress
Again the savage wilderness !
Blest if the desert's depths have wrought
For Freedom as thy deluge fought !

Teach us to front the tempest's gloom
With the long waves of light and bloom ;
To plant, where flashed the flying foam,
The constant altar-fires of home,
And the shrill sea-blast's wave prolong
In shepherd's bell and reaper's song !
To rear, by grace of grass and trees,
Of milky herds and honey-bees,
A second Holland from the seas.

GEORGIA.

BETWEEN her rivers and beside the sea,
My mother-land! What fairer land can be?

The lyric rapture in her leaping rills,
The crown-imperial on her purple hills.

Her lips are pure that never breathed a curse;
Her hands are white before the universe.

Behold the witness of the King of Peace
Clear, in the splendor of her dew-lit fleece.

And lo! the midnight of her shrouded *mine*
Garners the radiance of the years to shine.

Yea! the swart Gnome that bides his time below
Shall rise at last in full regalia glow!

And the great Alchemist shall teach the Sun
That Earth's great gloom and Life's great light are
        one!

Oh, sweetest souls that ever rose by prayer
White from the furnace-dungeon of despair!

That wrought new grace from battle's chaos-mould,
And reared new shrines from ashes not yet cold.

Not cold !—from flames the strangest that have given
From all this world, an altar-smoke to Heaven !

Crowned on the cross, above high-fetter line,
They smile on hate with Love's own smile divine.

Prouder than hills that plume thy star-ward crest,
Sweeter than dales that dimple at thy breast.

Richer than Rome ! when God's great chariot rolls,
Imperial Georgia ! count thy children's souls.

THE CONSTITUTION.

"LE ROI EST MORT !"

"AWAKE the King !" the warder said ;
"The night is past, the tempest fled.
Awake the King ; the world would shine
Once more beneath his eyes benign."

" The storm that rocked our castle's base
Brought heavy slumber to his Grace,
And light and peace and laughing skies
Shall wake him—" when the dead arise.

Ah ! deadlier than the tempest's peal,
In coward hands the traitor steel !
The Lord's anointed they that cried
"All hail !" have smitten, that he died.

They drank his cup, they brake his bread,
And in his slumber smote him dead,—
His loyal Lords!—to bear through time
The crimson of that banner crime!

On him all sacred seals were set;
In him all power and mercy met;
Dead! and *what* kings shall rise and reign
Ere we behold his like again!

ALEXANDER HAMILTON STEPHENS.

STONE MOUNTAIN.

FORGED in the furnace of the world's mid-fire;
Smit of all scourges of the fierce and dire;
Worn of all waters; the volcano's core
Enters the Heavens at last, triumphant evermore.

Crowned with the stars, a cenotaph to stand
Till the last flood of fire shall oversweep the land.
Kindred to all that, clasped by sod or shroud,
Kindles the crystal that shall cleave the cloud.

How vile to *this* the tyrant-triumph hid
In the worn Sphinx, the wasted pyramid!
How poor and pale all pomps the world has known
To this unblazoned shaft of Georgian stone!

5

Whose name and fame shall front the ages with
Thine awful grace, imperial monolith!
With fire as central as the planet's own,
And soul as steadfast as the granite stone?

Our Athos-Alexander, carven on
The unbowed head of mourning Macedon,
With crest of Memnon, by the choral seas,
Hymettus-voiced, with silvery symphonies.

Kindred to all that, swathed by sod or shroud,
Kindles the crystal that shall cleave the cloud;
Whose mighty work salutes the sun at last,
The rock cathedral of the fiery Past!

Shrining the princely dust with sacramental care,
And kindling darkened aisles with censer, song, and
        prayer;
Touching old banners with their battle-glow,
And the worn bugles till their triumphs blow;
Lending sweet music to the tears that shed
The tenderest splendor o'er our Freedom's dead,
And clarion clangors to the starward arch,
Where her gray cohorts rally to the march;
Blending all glories of the arch of light,
To robe, and crown, and consecrate the Right!

A kingly vigil, where enchantment lies
On the pale lips of peerless chivalries!
A godlike deed, to bid these charnel gates
Blaze with the resurrection of the States!

May we not mate the mountain and the man,—
The granite dome and the great Georgian?
Kindred to all that, clasped by sod or shroud,
Kindles the crystal that shall cleave the cloud.

Their pathos *one* !—the melancholy grace
Of Sinai's shadow on the prophet's face,
When the lone summit of the thunders saw
The broken people in the broken law,
And the last splendor of the lightning fell
On shattered tablets and lost Israel!

One in their grandeur!   Who shall bid apart
These stalwart coils that clasp our Georgia's heart?
Or crown this majesty that meets the sky
With other light of immortality
Than his, whose voice in Freedom's name hath given
From all this earth the noblest plea to Heaven?

"CORDELIA! CORDELIA!"

(IN MEMORIAM, APRIL 26, 1865.)

TO GENERAL ROBERT TOOMBS.

THE light hath lost its summer tints,
The world with woe hath whitened since
The shrouded April, long ago,
That laid our Lily in the snow !

The star that trembled down the west
Returns not from its quiet rest,
And if the dawn awake the flowers,
They shine for other eyes than ours !

And yet while grace of deed and thought
Shall linger where her hands have wrought,
We see the April of her eyes,
And wait her summer to arise.

Twin-born with liberty, she died
In the great battle, by her side,
Mute, save the proud appeal that lies
In silent lips and shrouded eyes.

The white palms crossed in perfect rest,
The Book of God upon her breast,
In witness of the good she sought,
In token that her task is wrought.

ARTHUR, THE GREAT KING.

TO JEFFERSON DAVIS.

THERE be of warders on the wall
Have heard by night his bugle-call,
And watchers ere the dawn unclose
Whose very tears are tint with rose.

As on some widowed neck the woe
Of mourning veils a whiter snow
Than April's first of whiteness, so
Across our path of murk and wrath
The clouds unclasp at times, and show
The vigil-gleam at "Camelot!"

His regal front is seamed and gaunt,
His kingly curls are grizzled, scant,
His war-steed worn to Rosinante!

There's mist upon his knightly mail,
And dust on every golden scale
Of the great "Dragon," crest to tail!

Like moonlit mist on midnight snow,
The sun of battle smoulders low!
Alas! the King at Camelot!

5*

But on his *sword* nor mould nor loss
From stainless steel to starry cross!
Ye wist, ye early at the tomb,
The whiteness that is like his plume!
Beloved of the morning-star,
Your eyes have seen "Excalibar!"

And ye that in the temples pray,
Have witnessed, when the aisles are gray,
A sudden rapture cleave the pane
Beyond the oriel's glory-stain,
That lingered in the holy place,
The "iris" of an angel's grace!
Then he whose head it kindled on
Shined like Uriel of the sun!
And were his face the Parian stone,
And were his smile King Arthur's own,
Of all that met his kindling eyes
Not one should marvel did he *rise!*

"These little ones!"—these lambs that bear
The dew-cross of our Christ; His care
These lilies, more than Eden blest,—
"These little ones" have touched his hem,
Have looked upon his diadem,
Have heard his footsteps walk with them,
And bring us, from the shrouded isle
Where his great glory bides the while,
The very sunshine of his smile!

And *One* I know, whose sabre shone
The battle's eye-light years agone,

Who wears upon his folded hands
The welcome of the angel lands,
And bears upon his smiling lips
The seal no shadow can eclipse,
Who waits me as the days expire
With *Arthur's* soul of love and fire !

———————

THE CAUCASIAN.

CHAINED to the icy peak,
Rent by the vulture's beak,
　Scourged of the bitter brine ;
Brother of Caucasus,
The gods have wrought on us
　Horrors to rival thine !

In the wilderness wreck we stand,
In the depths of the desolate land,
　To our dead in their graves we cry :
"Brothers ! that rest in peace
In the land where the wicked cease,
　Is it better to *live* or die ?"

And our dead from their graves reply :
" The Merciful moves on high.
　The arm of his strength is nigh,
In the sorrows that learn of Faith
To smile in the eye of Death.
　It is *braver* to live than to die !"

UNDER THE WILLOWS.

BRAVE "ends" may consecrate a cruel story,
  And crown a dastard deed ;
Brave hearts are laurelled with eternal glory
  That held another creed.

Who knows the end ? or in what record written
  The crowned results abide ?
The volume closed not with an Abel smitten
  Or Christ the crucified.

How poor and pale from yonder heights of Heaven
  Our Cæsar's pomp appears
To those who wear the purple robes of Stephen,
  Or Mary's crown of tears !

So let us watch, a single pale star keeping
  Its vigil o'er the tide.
No truth is *lost* for which the true are weeping,
  Nor *dead* for which they died.

ATLANTIS.

Down in the sunless deeps,
Our lost Atlantis sleeps !

Not as she sank below
The Deluge long ago,

A star for the bridal drest,
The glory of all the West,

But white in her shrouded rest,
And a chain across her breast.

Shall we weep while the waters roar,
Or *work* with the madrepore,

With the nursing fires below,
And the cradling earthquake's throe,

To lift to the light again
Atlantis, from shroud and chain

Slow dawning out of her grave,
Slow widening over the wave,

From the islet's slender spear
To the bloom of a hemisphere

Whose hills salute the morn
With the pomp of palm and corn,

Whose verdurous valleys shine
With the light of the oil and wine?

Ah! better than yonder hind,
Dazzled by triumph blind,

Whose share hath furrowed the sod
To hillocks that cry to God,

Whose scythe, as it sweeps the grain,
Shines with an evil stain,

To toil in the sunless deeps,
Where our lost Atlantis sleeps;

To tarry a thousand years
Till her Angel of Light appears.

DIXIE.

AIR—"ANNIE LAURIE."

Oh! Dixie's homes are bonnie,
  And Dixie's hearts are true;
And 'twas down in dear old Dixie
  Our life's first breath we drew;
  And there our last we'd sigh,
And for Dixie, dear old Dixie,
  We'll lay us down and die.

No fairer land than Dixie's
  Has ever seen the light;
No braver boys than Dixie's
  To stand for Dixie's right;
  With hearts so true and high,
And for Dixie, dear old Dixie,
  To lay them down and die.

Oh! Dixie's vales are sunny,
  And Dixie's hills are blue;
And Dixie's skies are bonnie,
  And Dixie's daughters, too,
  As stars in Dixie's sky;
And for Dixie, dear old Dixie,
  We'd lay us down and die.

*   *   *   *   *

No more upon the mountain,
   No longer by the shore,—
The trumpet song of Dixie
   Shall shake the world no more ;
For Dixie's songs are o'er,
   Her glory gone on high,
And the brave who bled for Dixie
   Have laid them down to die.

———

LOYAL.

[TO GENERAL CLEBURNE.]

THE good Lord Douglas—dead of old—
   In his last journeying
Wore at his heart, encased in gold,
   The heart of Bruce, his king,

Through Paynim lands to Palestine—
   For so his troth was plight—
To lay that gold on Christ his shrine,
   Let fall what peril might.

By night and day, a weary way
   Of vigil and of fight,
Where never rescue came by day,
   Nor ever rest by night.

And one by one the valiant spears
   Were smitten from his side,

And one by one the bitter tears
  Fell for the brave that died ;

Till fierce and black around his track
  He saw the combat close,
And counted but the single sword
  Against uncounted foes.

He drew the casket from his breast,
  He bared his solemn brow !
Oh, foremost of the kingliest !
  Go "first in battle" now !

Where leads my Lord of Bruce, the sword
  Of Douglas shall not stay !
Forward ! We meet at Christ His feet
  In Paradise, to-day !

The casket flashed ; the battle clashed,
  Thundered, and rolled away ;
And dead above the heart of Bruce
  The heart of Douglas lay !

Loyal ! Methinks the antique mould
  Is lost, or theirs alone
Who sheltered Freedom's heart of gold,
  Like Douglas, with their own !

THE HIELAND LASS AT LUCKNOW.

"DINNA YE HEAR THE PIBROCH?"

Not alone, not alone upon Lucknow's moan
   The midnight of blackness fell;
Not alone, not alone by her shattered stone,
   Stood Sorrow, the sentinel.
Not a heart but beat to her watcher's feet,
   Under that awful sky,
And ne'er a hearth on the darkened earth
   But blazed at the slogan's cry.

For the Campbells came like the rush of flame,
   With that clamor so wild and high,
That its clarion breath in the ears of Death
   Might have trembled with victory.
Here's a brimming can to the Highlandman,
   And the Bengal bolt he hurled!
Here's a brimming glass to the Hieland lass
   Who echoed it round the world!

"HONOR THE BRAVE."

UP in the Indian hills
  Of the Cutchee tribe 'tis said
That when a chieftain dies
  They bind his wrist with thread :
Green for the very brave ;
  But for the *bravest*, red.

One time in Indian wars,
  A squad of Englishmen
Charged sixty Cutcheears
  So valiantly that, when
The fight was done, of ten, not one
  Ever came back again.

Long after, when the winds
  Their skeletons had kissed,
A squad of Englishmen
  Looked up their missing list,
And found them dead, with each a thread
  Of scarlet on his wrist.

BATTLE FOR THE RIGHT.

"Oh! for the battle where all in all
Is placed on the perilous cast."
" Marks of Burhamville."

THEN smite, if thy foes are 'round thee,
And thou battlest for the right ;
Though the laurel hath ne'er crowned thee,
Thou art victor if thou smite !
But not in thy dreams Elysian
Thou speedest the battle on,
Not in the sleeper's vision
Is the victory lost or won.

Each blow for the truth thou givest
Is a triumph in the war,
Each hour that thou *truly* livest
Thou art truly Conqueror.
Each night of thy sinless slumber
That hails the setting sun,
Thy destiny shall number
As one brave victory won.

"SANS CHANGE."

FROM THE SEAL-RING OF BISHOP B——.

An earl of England hath as "crest"
An Infant in an Eagle's nest;

And (hid to heraldry) the strange
Yet simple legend, "Without change."

No herald; yet I hold amiss
The reading that traverses *this*.

No doubt the Eagle caught away
The Infant from its nurse that day,

And felt new softness at the touch,
Pervade his fiery spirit; much

As might the Lion that relents,
A Lamb, to Una's innocence.

And well, methinks, the nursling might
From the stern rapture of that flight

Some token of the eyrie bring
In dauntless eye and tireless wing;

6*

And so through annals richly stored,
Of gown, of mitre, and of sword,

Transmit, "unchanged," to all his race
The Eagle's fire, the Infant's grace.

AGONISTES.

BETWEEN the pillars let him stand !
The fireless eyes, the fettered hand,
The Lion-Fox that vexed the land !

By Baal ! but the sport was rare
To take the cunning in our snare,
The Lion, by his yellow hair !

The world grows weary of the jest,
And there are shadows in the west ;
Between the pillars let him rest !

Perhaps to dream, as captives will,
That on Philistia's sacred hill
His feet of triumph trample still.

To-morrow,—be the darkness short !—
Refreshed in rage, our gentle court
Shall bait the Titan for our sport !

So Peace, from pinnacle to porch,
With naked bone or blazing torch
Never more to smite or scorch !

And there was peace; and we have read
The simple prayer the captive said,
The blind man as he bowed his head;

And when the voice of other wail
Is still in story, let the tale
Of Agonistes turn us pale.

DIOGENES.

HE may have been a worthy wight
Who mocked the sun with candle-light,

As seeking in that foolish way,
An *honest man* in open day;

But who has heard of one of these
Revealed unto Diogenes?

I think his lanthorn lacked alone
Some honest motions of his own!

The man with little love shall find
But little loving in mankind;

And one of feeble honor can
By no means find an honest man!

To win the Indies' wealth, lay out
The Indies' worth, or thereabout.

"BARRY" OF ST. BERNARD.

TWELVE thousand feet, straight up the sky!
    Six thousand years of sleet!
Strange eyrie of humanity,
    With Europe at its feet!

How many a year the glacier,
    Slow gliding, shall not tell,
Since storms that launch the avalanche
    Have shouted as it fell.
There war's records rest in cloven crest
    And splintered pinnacle.

How many years, in deadliest wrath
    Of Roman and of Frank,
The red high-tide of murder hath
    Smitten this mountain's flank!

And this poor dog, his kennel, ice,—
    Ringed by the double strife,—
In his sublime self-sacrifice
    Stands staunch for human life!

Lead out your kings! an even start
    For Glory's last reward!
Your Hannibal, your Bonaparte,
    Your Cæsar, evil-starred,
And here's my "vote," with all my heart,
    For "Barry" of Bernard.

Climb the fierce legions as of old
   Storm swept and battle riven !
And as the foremost hearts fall cold
The Alps, by all their height, uphold
   A dog, the nearest Heaven !

THE PRISONER AT GLATZ.

FROM THE LIFE OF FREDERICK WILLIAM III., OF PRUSSIA.

One in his palace : *One* at the bars
Of a dungeon, under the Alpine stars ;
Doomed ! and never hath dungeon's scope
Closed on a darker farewell to hope.

Years ! and ever that icy gleam ;
Years ! and only the eagle's scream,
Piercing the storm in its sunward flight,
Hath cheered his soul at that awful height.

He hath barred his soul at a deadlier height
With icier bonds, but they melt to-night.

Not for the hopes that have vanished dim ;
Not for the pang of the fettered limb ;
Other than anguish has melted him,
That fell with a light from the starry dome
On a single line in an ancient tome,
" In the time of thy trouble, call thou on *Me ;*
And, lo ! my love shall deliver thee !"
And his soul is bowed like a bended knee.

And his tears are wept from a heart as full
As the night of stars, with the beautiful
Child-like trust in the Merciful.

One in his palace—the balm of night,
With the beautiful sleep, hath fled his sight,
Sick and faint with the woe and weight
Of the golden thorns that crown the great—
Moans, as the stricken who moan for light
In the dark " mid-watch," and at dawn, for night :

" All my realm for the sweet release
From a monarch's pain to a peasant's peace !"

A soft step stole through the silken gloom,
A sweet voice read from " ancient tome"—
Sweeter sounds may not lull the sense—
Of the pitying love and the innocence
Of Christ ; and there came the sweep
Of angel pinions, and brought him sleep !

One in his palace, the dawn astir,
Saith to his sweet-voiced Comforter :

" All my realm by the east and west,
All my glory, hath never blessed
My soul like this great crown-jewel *Rest !*

" Tell me now of the heaviest woe
That dwells to-day with my deadliest foe ;

" For, as the Lord hath regarded me,
My soul would pardon mine enemy."

And the soft voice answered, " The sorrow that's
Under the icy stars, at *Glatz !*"

Aye !   There are pinions of farther flight
Than the eagle's scream or the Alpine height
To answer the captive's call to-night !

Mercy !—waiting, through *all* our years,—
Waiting one signal, one summons, *Tears !*

"FELIX."

THERE is an ancient moral,
   Whose pith I thus convey,—
Who slumbers on his laurel
   Was vanquished yesterday.

Though greener fields may brighten
   Than yet the sun hath known ;
Though whiter harvests whiten
   Than ever seed were sown ;

Above the breast of summer,
   The thunder-bolt may burst ;
And around the sheaves of harvest
   The winter gales are nursed.

Life's loftiest triumph trembles
   Beneath the lightest march,—
Till Death, that carves the keystone
   Writes FELIX on the arch.

SONGS OF HOME.

7
73

.

A SONG FOR THE ASKING.

(TO R. N. T.)

A SONG !   What songs have died
    Upon the earth,
Voices of Love and Pride—
    Of Tears and Mirth?
Fading as hearts forget,
    As shadows flee !
Vain is the voice of song,
       And yet
       I sing to thee !

A song !   What ocean shell
    Were silent long,
If in thy touch might dwell
    Its all of song ?
A song ?   Then near my heart
    Thy cheek must be,
For, like the shell, it sings—
       Sweet Heart—
       To Thee, of Thee !

TO ROSALIE.

How shall I sing to thee?
What shall the measure be,
Star of my reverie,
Loveliest Rosalie,
          Purest of Pearls?
·Smooth as thy forehead fair?
Sweet as thine eyelids are?
          Soft as thy curls?

As from the starry vines
Of the white jessamines,
When the first planet shines,
          Only at even,
Incense, the wanton day
Vainly would woo away,
Freed from the bending spray,
          Rises to Heaven.

As in the forest dim,
Cradled in mossy rim,
Murmurs the fountain's hymn,
          Seeking no river;
Lulling the lily's sleep,
Watching the shadows creep,
          And the stars quiver;
Such should my measure be,

Such were my minstrelsie,
Maid of my reverie
Sacred and sweet *to thee*,
Or silent forever.

AN APRIL MORNING.

A DEEPER azure where the clouds are flying
Along the upper sky,
A softer shadow where the leaves are lying
Our forest pathway by,
A sweeter murmur in the south winds sighing,
Tell us the spring is nigh.

The blue-bird flits, and coos the ring-dove tender
Amid the young green leaves;
Mansions of mist and silver, white and slender,
The shy wood-spider weaves;
Swingeth the swallow to his old home under
The unforgotten eaves.

Its bridal wreaths, with starry gems of yellow,
The jasmine's stores unfold,
Adown the tresses of the trembling willow
Dropping its bells of gold;
Fit tracery to deck the perfumed pillow,
Where Love's young dreams are told.

A thousand forms, like frolic children hiding,
Challenge the laughing showers,

Watching the flight of pearly clouds and chiding
  The treasure-laden hours;
A thousand forms of untold beauty biding
  Amid the unborn flowers.

A thousand forms, and not in nature only,
  The warm spring showers unfold,
Another mission, pure and calm and holy,
  The voice of spring has told,
Waking some joy in souls long sad and lonely,
  Some hope in hearts long cold.

Some light from sunlight may our sadness borrow,
  Some strength from bright young wings,
Some hope from brightening seasons, when each morrow
  A lovelier verdure brings;
Some softened shadow of remembered sorrow
  From the calm depths of springs.

Blend thy blest visions with the sleep that cumbers
  The dull, cold earth so long;
Bring bloom and fragrance to the flow'ret's slumbers,
  And bid our hearts be strong;
Breathe thine own music through our spirit's numbers,
  Season of light and song.

TWILIGHT ON "TORCH HILL."

IT is eve at our eyrie ; the river
    Falls dim in its tremulous gaze ;
There's a mantle of mist and the quiver
    Of stars through the violet haze.

Soft twilight ! the far silent city
    Sleeps, veiled in the valley beneath,
Eclipsed by the flash of this pretty
    Bright " ruby-throat"* here on his wreath.

Shall I try, ere the daylight is over,
    So high from its dust and its din,
How much of a "*town*" I can cover
    With the leaf of a jessamine ?

All the life and the light of the city
    Shall I daintily hide from my sight,
With its sorrow that weeps, and the pity
    That walks with the angels to-night ?

Sweet mercies that shadow me ! Never !
    Lest the soul in my body should die,
Ere the sparkle fades out of the river,
    Or the light from the violet sky.

* The ruby-throated humming-bird, avant-courier of the stars.

"DO THEY MISS ME AT HOME?"

"The world is not all so dark
But a smile can make it sweet."
TENNYSON.

A QUESTION that betrays
The answer ere it come,
For that " I miss" conveys
That I *am* missed at home.

For so the world is full
Of call that answers call,
Along the wires that pull
Both ways or not at all.

AMONG THE BIRDS.

WE built a nest among the birds
   Now many Mays ago ;
And we have heard a many a word
   That sang, by building so.

And times when dew is on the day,
   And starlight in the trees,
We meet and warn the mists away
   With little lays like these :

A birdie tells of dimpled dells
   That blushed in far-off springs ;
And many an April blooms and thrills
   With rapture while she sings.

A birdie coos of light and shade
   The summers brought our nest,
Of violets born, and lilies laid
   Where lilies love to rest.

A birdie carols : Day's decline
   Restores the dawn's caress ;
And autumn pours a richer wine
   Than April's tenderness.

A birdie says: The bitter days
  May blow till they expire;
The winds but raise our censer blaze
  And waft its incense higher!

The birdies sing: The bright shells bring
  No song from all the sea;
The close cheek and the clasping hand
  Make life's whole melody.

"IN MAMRE."

Do you ever think when your Eden-tree
  Is flourishing wide and green,
With friendships thicker than fruits of gold,
  And love with its flowers between,
How many beautiful souls may be
  That your soul hath never seen?
And how much "loving" your heart could hold
Were the blossoms silver, the apples gold,
  And your heart an evergreen?

In a world so wide there are nooks to hide,
  And shadows to veil the sweet;
And there are the wise with unseeing eyes,
  And the swift with unheeding feet.
Happier we, were our Eden-tree
  A tent in the desert's heat,
Who hold that the very angel who spoke

To Abraham, under the Mamre oak,
  May be the next we meet !

'Tis a pleasant thought at the eventide,
  When a glory looks down on our prayers,
That we have not mocked in the days of our pride
The meanest pilgrim whose dust may hide
  An "angel unawares !"
And a beautiful hope, as the night unrolls
  Her raiment of rest serene,
That we are nearer the beautiful souls
  That our souls have never seen.

IDYL.

(TO M. N. T.)

I.

A VISION which I had of late,
By the orchard's lattice gate,
Let this simple song relate !

Vision of a little girl,
With a cheek of peach and pearl,
And the promise of a curl !

Daintily in white arrayed,
Borne by Ethiopian maid,
Blending well with light and shade.

Dimpled hand on dusky neck,
Ebony with silver fleck,
'Twixt a turban and a check !

By the cedar's scented gloom,
By the violet's perfume,
By the jasmine's golden bloom,

By the graceful hawthorn tree,
By the stately hickory,
Pausing for a kiss from me !

Melting where the sunlight shines,
On the blossomed nectarines,
Melting down the orchard lines.

II.

Melts, but bids before me rise
A wiser pair of wider eyes,
In a wide world of surprise,

And a world of rapture swells
In her accent as she tells
All the legends of our dells.

Where the wild bee builds her cells,
Where the humming-birdie dwells,
Where the squirrel drops the shells !

Voice, by soul of music stirred,
Eloquent in tone and word,
Mocks the very mocking-bird.

And she knows the way of fruit,
All the tricks of bud and shoot,
All the secrets of the root.

Much that wiser folk call weeds
Her wide horticulture heeds;
Boundless her delight in seeds.

Leave her to her slender hoe,
Let the seasons come and go,
Let the flowers and maiden grow.

III.

Another Presence ! bright, yet pure,
With mien more modest than demure.
Not our little maiden, sure ?

Yes ! by dimpled cheek and chin,
Violet eyes, and velvet skin,
'Tis our "Summer-child" again !

'Mid the roses she hath wrought—
'Mid the lilies till she caught
Health and grace in form and thought.

Greet her, all ye clustered blooms !
Apples, peaches, pears, and plums,
Greet your sweetest as she comes !

By the cedar's scented breath,
By the violets underneath,
By the jasmine's golden wreath.

Crown her with your fragrant hands,
All bright things from all bright lands,
Crown your brightest, where she stands,

By the graceful hawthorn tree,
By the stately hickory,
Pausing for a kiss from me.

TO THE LITTLE ROSALIE.

(MRS. ROBERT OBER.)

A LITTLE leaf from the rose's heart,
  A little drop of pearl,
To write a little bit of a rhyme
  For a little bit of a girl !
Bright as a little humming-bird,
  Sweet as a honey-bee,
That all who sing to the flowers may sing
  To the little Rosalie !

The violet's dyes are in her eyes,
  Its softest velvet in
The dimples, the dimples about her cheeks,
  The dimple upon her chin !
Ah ! well of the little humming-bird,
  Ah ! well of the little bee,
To sing, to sing to as sweet a thing
  As the little Rosalie !

We think, we think of the starward palms
   Over the Orient seas,
We drink, we drink of the blended balms
   From the bright Hesperides.
We ask, we ask of the golden hours,
   Of blossom, and bird, and tree,
A little lyric of stars and flowers
   For the little Rosalie !

"MOTHER'S WORK."

DARNING stockings
   For restless feet,
Scrubbing faces
   To lily-sweet !
Teaching Bible
   And catechism,
Soothing bruises
   And healing schism.
      Smooth and smoother,
        Linger nor jerk ;
     That's our mother—
       The woman's work !

Raising roses,
   Burying smarts,
Hiving sunshine
   Under our hearts !

Bravest spirit
  Beneath the dome !
Dastards falter
  When *she says* " Come !"
    Smooth and smoother,
      " Nor haste nor rest !"
    Beautiful mother,
      Whom God hath blest.

Tender, most tender !
  Child, take heed !
Rare her splendor
  Of thought and deed.
Mild as moonlight
  In softest quiver,
To shine with the stars
  Forever and ever !
    Smooth and smoother—
      When life hath flown—
    The wings of " Mother"
      Still woo our own.

GROUP OF DUCKLINGS.

DUCKLINGS, six of the downiest
That a duck could hatch if she did her best,
Or a painter paint at his creamiest.

Of the richest and roliest-poliest;
First choice Frank's! and the present quest
Of Frank's forefinger "the prettiest!"

Round and round, as a hawk that eyes
Ducklings, *six* of the dumpling size;
Each *so* suitable—still she flies.

Ducklings, six, and *one* for dinner!
But which? so hovers the dainty sinner,
Nor fills the hollow that acheth in her.

" *This* is the prettiest—brownie-white!
Except this yellow one on the right—
I mean the *left*—with a fly in sight."

"The one that scampers! The one that's *still!*
The one *afloat*, with dripping bill.
Prettiest, washed and had his fill!
But hungry Top-knot's prettier still!"

" *This* one! after the bug. The *other*,
Watching at once the bug and his brother!"
"Which *is* the prettiest?" "*Ask their mother!*"

Puzzled Frank ! I know a nest,
And a mother too of the wisest, best,
Who could not tell, and who would not test,
For the wide world at its happiest,
Which of her d—arlings she loves the best.

"WHIPPOORWILL."

WHIP POOR WILL ! Was there ever heard
Such a blood-thirsty, slanderous, scandalous bird !
Under the window so slyly to creep,
And whistle "come whip him" while Will's asleep.
It's a bird of darkness, and not of day,
That whistles a hint that he dare not say.

Whip Poor Will ! Why, what has he done ?
Has he found your eggs, ma'am, and broken one ?
Has he torn his jacket, or fought at play,
Or missed his lesson, or ran away,
Or broke a tumbler, or scratched the chairs,
Or choked at table, or spoke at prayers ?

No, Willie's a boy that's nice and neat,
And Willie's a boy that's bright and sweet ;
He's quiet at home and he's quick at school,
And he never breaks, if he knows, the rule ;
And I really think it were wondrous silly
For nothing at all to whip poor Willie !

But, Whippoorwill, if you've really seen
Another Willie that's bad and mean,
And you think you ought, and think 'twill " pay,"
To whip poor Willie, why whip away.
And so good-by to your birdship till
There's more occasion to whip *our* Will !

THE ECHO STORY.

THIS is a rhyme that our poet writ,
  Sitting at peace one day,
With his warring done, and his rifle-gun
  Bracketted away.

A little lad in the curly grace
  Of summers that numbered three,
With a wrathful trace on his rosy face,
  Stood at his mother's knee.

" Mother, get me a rifle-gun,
  With a bayonet keen and bright ;
There's a fellow that hides in the hills in front,
  And him I am bound to fight ! ·

" A fellow that hoots like a hooting owl,
  And mocks like a mocking-bird ;
A *rascal* that calls me the meanest names
  That ever a fellow heard.

" Now, mother, get me a rifle-gun,
     And a jacket of blue or gray,
And I think you'll hear of the prettiest fight,
     Or the funniest run-away!"

And the mother, parting the sunny curls,
     Smiled in the earnest eyes:
" I know the lad; he's of Johnny's age,
     And just about Johnny's size.

" He'll never run from your rifle-gun;
     We'll try him another way.
Speak lovingly to that lad, my son,
     And hear what he has to say."

Soon, in the porch that faced the hills,
     They stood in the waning light,
And a voice replied to the voice that cried,
     " Johnny, my dear, good-night!"

And Johnny's smile, as he turned away,
     Was audible, sweet, and clear;
And it was a rather good thing to say,
     And a very good thing to hear.

And I hope the world as it grows in grace
     Will learn how a war is won;
That Love is still the invincible,—
     And bracket its rifle-gun.

POETA IN RURE.

Now, doth it give the corn a start,
　Or cause the cotton grow?
They mock the minstrel's idle art
　My neighbors of the hoe;
With rumble of the tumble cart,
　And lyric of "Gee-Whoa!"

Their legends are of doughty teams,
　Of oxen and of sheep;
I hear them driving in their dreams
　And counting in their sleep.

And yet their wit is rich in speech,
　The wisest, uninspired;
Their limbs unto the fiddle screech
　Right rhythmically wired.

Within these fields of care and strife
　A man may come, no doubt,
To be a poet, all his life,
　And never find it out.

To dwell among his woolly flocks,
　His herds of hoof and horn,
Less happy than the licensed "ox
　That treadeth out the corn!"

To hold the sky in all its scope
  As one great weather-sign,
To toil athwart the vineyard's slope
  And never taste the wine !

The day must have its dinner-gong,
  The nation must be fed,
Yet one *will* weary of a song
  With one sole burden, *bread.*

And one must count his labor " naught,"
  His harvest quite in vain,
Who reared no blossom when he wrought
  With summer on the plain,
No garland of a golden thought
  To glorify his grain.

THE FLOWERS.

A BLESSING on the broad bright lands,
  Whose children come to ours,
And lead us with their fragrant hands
  Around the World of Flowers.

No dust upon our sandalled feet,
  As they who go to find
In other lands a flower as sweet
  As one they left behind.

With them our thoughts all journeys take,
  With them our fancies roam,
And ever when we *will* we *wake*
  And find ourselves at home.

They bid the green oasis creep
  Around the desert wells;
They sound on many a cedared steep
  The sweet pagoda bells.

They wake for us the breath and bloom
  Where soft Circassia smiles;
They veil beneath their tender bloom
  The maidens of the Isles.

All times and climes they journey through,
  Until their pathway lies
Beyond the gates of Morning, to
  The walks of Paradise.

And many an angel of the earth
  Their upward path hath trod,
Gone from our garden gateways forth
  Into the arms of God.

THE PEDLER MAN AT TORCH HILL.

POETS and pedlers!   From the early day
  Till now the night of "letters" closes blind,
Pedlers and poets on the king's highway
  Have met, with salutations quaint though kind.

Who walks with Wordsworth, or with Shakspeare's
        wings
  Winnows the gold from this world's dusty cares,
May glean a grace from life's most common things,
  And entertain an angel unawares.

In thoughts like these my inner man rejoiced,
  As nightfall dropped a pedler at the gate,
A huge " bed-tick" upon his shoulder hoist,
  A thousand pounds—in size, if not in weight.

The house-dog silenced, from the gate I heard
  The olden plaint of all the world's highways:
" Footsore and hungry!" though, I wis, no word
  Of retrospective hint at " better days!"

" A plague on pedlers!" is the form of wish
  With which one's pedler welcome should begin ;
Which, as a poet, I condensed to " Pish!"
  And bade the biped dromedary in.

And in he came; at every step a bow
   That offered me the mattress on his back,
As one by duty doubly bent—to show
   His weight of obligation and of pack.

Much talk, but none that I might understand;
   Of plaintive demonstration, also, much.
I only gathered that his Faderland
   Was farther off,—Jerusalem or Dutch!

Some arrant knight of commerce, who hath strayed
   To these poor parts, by cheating fancy led,
To drive a brief but profitable trade
   In lies and linen tapes, thieving and thread;

In drill-eyed sharps, no sharper than himself,
   'Tho' dull his eye and all adust his skin;
To plunder pity of her slender pelf,
   And thrive in chief when chiefly "taken in."

His supper done, I him to bed allowed;
   But soon thereafter, passing unawares,
I saw (and beg your pardon if I bowed
   And said "Amen") the pedler at his prayers!

I do not deem all pedlers are devout;
   I do not argue that they all are Dutch;
I only urge the pressure of the doubt
   To hold in reasonable honor such.

"GELERT."

'TWAS not for special beauty,
　Though beautiful was he,
Nor yet in reverent honor
　Of a stainless pedigree,
That reached across the ocean,
　Through twice a century.

But for love that ever listened
　To affection's lightest breath,
For a faithfulness that glistened
　In the very haze of death,
That our cedars droop their shadows,
　And our jasmines twine a wreath.

Under the great Deodar
　There lies a little mound,—
As beneath some proud pagoda
　A prince might slumber sound,
In the verdure and the odor
　Of consecrated ground,—
And a hand hath written "Gelert"
　In honor of a hound.

·HOME.

FOREST-GIRDED, cedar-scented,
   Veiled like Vesper, sweet and dim ;
Pure as burned the Temple's glory,
   Shadowed by the Seraphim ;
Islet from contending oceans,
   Coral-cinctured, crowned with palm,
Where the wrestling world's commotions
   Melt through music into calm ;
Throats that sing and wings that flutter
   Softly 'mid the balm and bloom ;
Sweeter sounds than lip can utter
   Hath my heart for thee,
       My home.

Bless that dear old Angel Saxon
   For the sounds he formed so well ;
Little words, the nectar-waxen
   Harvest of a honey-cell,
Sealing all a summer's sweetness
   In a single syllable !
For, of all his quaint word-building,
   The queen-cell of all the comb
Is that grand old Saxon mouthful,
   Dear old Saxon *heartful*,
       Home.

POEMS OF SENTIMENT AND HUMOR.

"NINA"—HER EYES.

I KNOW the summers that can speak
For all the olive of thy cheek;
I know the gentle lineage rare
That crowns thy head with midnight hair;
But whence—don't send me to the skies!—
The splendor, Nina, of your eyes?

Now, Nina, there's your needle! Knit!
Your lashes drooped a little bit;
I'm writing "letters," and afraid
Of brilliant cross-lights; lend me shade.
Nay! there's a dimple at your lips,
And there—you dazzle, past eclipse!

Was it of much or little "grace"
To mock these clouds of commonplace
With a whole summer sunset's dyes,
Because you *must* lift up your eyes?
Sending my missive all amiss,
Turning my "letter" into *this!*

You couldn't help it! Once, amid
A temple's twilight, it betid
The soft glow of a vestal's light
Slept on the crosslet of a knight,

And wrought—nor, Nina, might it less
Of loyalty and tenderness—
The matchless radiance that lies
Deep in the splendor of your eyes!

TO THE LITTLE LADY ALICE.

No *dew* distils on Georgia's hills,
   Or eke Circassia's valleys,
That leaves a pearl on lily's curl
         As pure as Lady Alice!
My lily-pet! my violet!
         My little Lady Alice!

As rare as rise through Southern skies
   Aurora-boreales!
As rare as *rose* on Northern snows,
   Or heart's-ease in a palace,
Is she, my sprite! my brownie bright!
         My little Lady Alice!

The wise old Greek his fate might seek,
   And bear his foes no malice;
And so might I, my idol's eye,
   If *you* but bore the chalice,
And drink to thee in three times three,
         My little Lady Alice!
My heart's delight! my star of night!
My perfect little chrysolite!
         My little Lady Alice!

BROWNIE BELLE, OF THE ESQUILINE.

(ON HER RETURN FROM EUROPE.)

WHERE the almond blossoms first,
Where the nectarines are nursed,
Grew with cedar and with pine,
Grew with violet and vine,
   With her brows of calm,
With her eyes divine,
   With her breath of balm,
And her blush like wine,
Brownie Belle, of the Esquiline.

     Grew in grace,
  Like the blue Glycine;
     Grew in grace,
  Like a jessamine;
     In stateliness,
  Like a Norfolk pine;
     With a tender gloom
  In her eyes divine,
     And an olive bloom
  Through her blush like wine;
     Grew in grace,—
  And I knew the girl,
     From her dancing foot
  To her floating curl.

Grew in grace,—
And I knew her well,
From the honey-dew
To the nectar-cell ;
From the morning mist,
Till the manna fell
On the tents, the *lips*
Of Israel.

In stateliness, like the star of trees
With the silver lace, from the Indian seas,
When the silver mist
And the stars are met
On her coronet ;
On the stately crest of the stateliest
Star-lit Tree-star,
Bright Deodar.

Sweet the air of the Esquiline,
From morning prayer till nuts and wine ;
Where the dancing gods of days divine
Might dance on sods embroidered fine
With the richest tints of the ripest wine
Of every land where the sun doth shine.

We'll gather all
Of the bright and sweet ;
We'll lay them all
At our Brownie's feet.
We'll gather all for a garland feast,
When the stars recall *our* star from the East.
When she comes, she comes

With her balm and bloom ;
And the tender gloom
Of her eyes shall shine
To crown the lights of the Esquiline.

"SUNBEAM."

(TO MISS E. V. C.)

It was an old philosopher,
And also very wise,
That had a little "prism"
And specs before his eyes ;
And he caught a little sunbeam
That he would analyze.

It was a rare philosopher
That labored days and nights,
And split his little sunbeam
Into—seven—lights ;
And he blessed his specs and prism
That showed such lovely sights.

And he gathered mighty glory
For doing little more
Than a little drop of water
Had often done before ;
And his name, 'twas Newton, kindles
'Till the light shall shine no more.

Ah! had he caught the sunbeam
    Our poet saw one day,
He would have split his prism,
    And thrown his specs away;
A dew-drop could have shown him
    More colors to the ray.

Our poet keeps no prism
    Nor other glasses, yet
His simple optics sundered,
    'Twixt pearl and violet,
At least a half a hundred,
    And he is counting yet!

TO A LADY OF TEXAS, IN ITALY.

(MRS. WILLIAM MAVERICK.)

A THOUSAND leagues of steam and foam,
To breathe, tho' but an hour, in Rome!
To wake in Florence, or to be
Cradled in Venice by the sea!
Yet sometimes, lady, when thine eyes
Are weary of yon wondrous skies,
With all thy pulses languid grown
To miracles in stain and stone,
Seek thou some sacred fountain dim,
A mirror with its marble rim,
And bend thy "sunbeam" face to see
The fairest thing in Italy!
Yea, lovelier than the sunset seas
Kindled, to guide the Genoese!

TO —— ——

WHAT! must the glowing heart forbear
    Its homage to the skies,
When all the glories wandering there
    But wake to win our eyes?
Shall earth come forth in vain to wear
    Her robe of endless dyes,
And not to aught of bright or fair
    Our adoration rise?
Nay, from the sternest soul would steal
The homage it could not conceal.

The stars with but a lovelier ray
    Our lowly homage bless;
And earth receives with smiles more gay
    Our debt of thankfulness.
Then why the deep emotion stay,
    The burning words repress,
That fill the worship we would pay
    To woman's loveliness?
As pure as Heaven, than earth more fair,
How dark the soul that bows not there!

THE BRIDE.

HER eyes are bright as stars that keep
　Their watch in midnight skies;
Her voice as sweet as winds that sweep
　The harps of Paradise.
And thou must quench the starry rays
　That make the midnight fair,
Ere thou canst teach the heart to gaze
　And not to worship there.

Learn, if thou wilt, from wisdom's store,
　The stoic's boasted art;
And lose, like him, the only lore
　That could have cheered thy heart.
Then *die*, for life hath naught of bloom
　Around thy path to shine;
And death can bring no deeper gloom
　To souls so dark as thine.

THE BROWN BRIDGE.

THE brown bridge spans the streamlet, and
The evergreens from hand to hand
Arch the roadway's snow-white sand.

A picture ! and I loved the same
Till Annie there to meet me came
And turned my picture to a frame,

An oval, such as might entwine
The mild Madonna of a shrine
From some old master's hand divine.

And ever since, in passing there,
The same sweet phantom haunts the air
With azure eyes and golden hair.

Grow on, ye evergreens, and throw
Soft shadows on the dust below !
And ye dark waters murmur low

Of *other* streams, not dark or wide,
So Annie with the grace that died
Shall meet me on the other side.

THE VALLEY OF NACOOCHEE.

"EVENING STAR."

CHILD of our Chattahoochee,
  Hid in the hills afar;
Oh! beautiful Nacoochee,
  Light of the Evening Star!

Smile of the dreaming maiden,
  Song of the bird's release;
Grace of the blest in Aidenne,
  Valley of light and peace.

Clasped in the mountain shadows,
  The May dew on her breast,
Her breath is the balm of meadows,
  Her *name* is a hymn to "Rest."

The voice of a loved one calling
  To feet that have wandered far:
Return, for the night is falling;
  Rest with the Evening Star.

THE HALL.

(PAGE BROOK.)

THERE is dust on the door-way, there is mould on
    the wall;
There's a chill at the hearth-stone, a hush through
    the hall;
And the stately old mansion stands darkened and cold
By the leal loving hearts that it sheltered of old.

No light at the lattice, no gleam from the door;
No feast on the table, no mirth on its floor;
But "Glory departed" and silence alone.
"Dust unto dust" upon pillar and stone.

No laughter of childhood, no shout on the lawn;
No footstep to echo the feet that are gone:
Feet of the beautiful, forms of the brave,
Failing in other lands, gone to the grave!

No carol at morning, no hymn rising clear;
No song at the bridal nor chaunt at the bier.
All the chords of its symphonies scattered and riven;
Its altar in ashes, its incense in Heaven!

Is there pæan for Glory, whose triumph shall stand
By the wreck of a home once the pride of the land?

Its chambers unfilled as its children depart,
The melody stilled in its desolate heart!

Yet the verdure shall creep to the mouldering wall,
And the sunshine shall sleep in the heart of "The
    Hall;"
And the foot of the pilgrim shall find till the last
Some fragrance of Home at this shrine of the Past.

THE OLD HARPSICHORD.

"In one room of this deserted mansion we came upon an old harp-
sichord with a single unbroken string. Evoking the last sound from
it, we extracted the key, which you will find herewith."—*Letter from
the Old Dominion.*

WHAT of the night, old sleeper?
    What of thy watch so lone?
Of the darkness and dust, and deeper,
    The silence that shrouds thine own?
What song for the tuneless Reaper
    Who binds all songs in one?
Crown thou his sheaf, oh sleeper!
    With a requiem monotone!

One chord in thy heart unbroken!
    One key to that chord alone!
A touch—and thy thought hath spoken;
    A sigh—and thy song hath flown!
A sigh for the single token
    Of all who have sung and flown!

Of symphonies ceased forever ;
  Of harmonies heard no more ;
Of chords that have ceased to quiver
  Or ever thy task was o'er :
Songs and their symphonies never
  Dying in requiems more.

Silence and darkness blended,
  Dust on a desolate shore,
Footprints of angels ascended
  Around us forevermore !
When the lips of the beautiful singers
  With the silvery chords lie low,
And only an echo lingers
  Of the melodies sweet and old,
To blend 'neath their seraph fingers
  With a hymn from their harps of gold.

THE COLONNADE.

A STILLNESS in the lonely hall,
A shadow on the vacant wall,
A broken hearth, an incense flown,
And dust upon the altar-stone ;
What deeper gloom to match the shade
That wraps the lonely Colonnade ?

White roses round the columns cling,
White moonbeams in the flow'r may fling
A mingled shadow, when appear
The lost of many a lonely year,

In phantom forms, that meet and fade
Along the lonely Colonnade.

No more beneath the moonlit leaves
The evening star its song receives;
For many golden chords are riven
That sent that twilight song to heaven,
And scattered far the feet that strayed
Along the lonely Colonnade.

No more in murmured tones rehearse
The hero's tale, the lover's verse,
Nor voice of song, nor sigh of flute,
Where lips of sweeter tone are mute;
Oh, lips! that loving hands have laid
Far from the lonely Colonnade.

Oh, sister! if the past imparts
But dreams of sadness to our hearts,
Why ask we of the coming years
A better blessedness than tears,
Amid the pale white flowers arrayed
Along life's lonely Colonnade?

THE HILLS.

I.

BELOW the granite chain
Appalachian,
Above the sandy plain,
Which under-dips the main,
   There lies a belt of hills,
   Which the Middle Georgian tills.

The hills! and how came they?
The yellow, red, and gray?
The gravel, sand, and clay?
The big ones, why so tall?
The little ones, so small?
How came they here at all?
   Is the mystery that fills
   The history of the hills,
   With much perplexity
   For my geology.

Whether deposited
In the deep ocean's bed,
As one might softly spread
An ancient feather-bed
Over an earthquake's head.
Till waking with a shout,
The giant laid about,
And made a hill "crop out"

For every deadly blow
Delivered down below.

Or whether 'twas the gift
(A most prodigious lift!)
Of the era known as "drift,"
When the ice-raft stole away
The gravel, sand, and clay
From many an Arctic bay,
And "bowlder," by the way,
Bore southward day by day
Till on the floor it lay,—
  On the grooved and furrowed floor
Of the slow-receding sea,—
And, cracking with a roar,
Poured mud from every pore,
To make one hillock more,
  Which the slow-receding sea,
With its softly-lapping hands
Amid the moistened sands,
    Like a man that undertakes
    To mould before he bakes,
    Or a child that patti-cakes,—
Which the slow-receding sea,
With its softly-dimpled hands,
With its foam-white ruffled hands,
With its diamonded hands,
    Bequeathed as "Cotton-Lands"
    To all the world—to me,
    And my Geology,
    A much perplexi—T.

II.

"The hills, and how came they?"
We pondered yesterday;
As one who rhymes his way
    Through the mystery that fills
    The history of hills—
    The everlasting hills—
With an everlasting doubt
As to how they came about.

To a metre not more slow,
To a measure that must flow
To the echo of a woe,
We rhyme again to show
The hills, and *where they go.*
Their coming none may know,
Nor question *where they go !*

Oh, brothers ! shall the land
Which our loving Father planned
For the honest heart and hand,—
The hills our Father planned,
And with softest seasons spanned,
Which he gathered from the sea,
And gave to you and me,—
Hear the echo of the woe,
"The hills ! and *here they go*
To the ocean, whence they sprung,
Bewept, and *not unsung !*"
My brothers, answer No !

The hills!   We love the hills.
Their heads are nearest Heaven,
Their sides to morn and even !
    There is a joy that fills
    Their anthem to the day ;
    There is a peace that fills
    The requiem of hills
    To the light that dies away.
'Tis more than song or wine
To see their summits shine,
Through twilight's purple wine,
    Like islands of the blest,
    In the ocean of their rest ;
When the broad palm of the sun,
With his signet-star thereon,
Is raised in benison,
    " Hold fast the hills below !
    Your hills and homes, and so
    Until the dark be light,
    God bless you, and good-night !"

JUNIALUSKEE.

(A FAMOUS SOUTHERN APPLE OF INDIAN ORIGIN.)

WHERE shall the red man rest at last, that the white
    man shall not find him?
Where shall his wigwam smoke arise, nor draw his
    "fate" behind him?
Where shall he plant an apple-seed that a pale-face
    shall not gather
The golden fruit ere the downward root hath tapped
    the Indian's father?

Under his spreading apple-tree, to his sons and daugh-
    ters dusky,
With their heads bowed down to their travel-gear,
    spoke Chieftain Junialuskee.
His sons and daughters are on their way, and Junia-
    luskee follows.
And his apple-tree? Why Junialus*kee* sold it for fifty
    dollars!

NANTAHALEE.

You've heard, I think, of the beautiful maid
   Who fled from Love's caresses,
Till her beautiful toes were turned to roots,
And both her shoulders to beautiful shoots,
And her beautiful cheeks to beautiful fruits,
   And to blossoming spray her tresses !

I've *seen* her, man ! she's living yet
   Up in a Cherokee valley !
She's an apple-tree ! and her name might be,
In the softly-musical Cherokee,
   A long-drawn " Nantahalee !"
'Tis as sweet a word as you'll read or write ;
Not *quite* as fair as the *thing*, yet quite
Sufficient to start an old anchorite
Out of his ashes to bless and *bite*
   The beautiful " Nantahalee !"

FABLE.

NOT IN ÆSOP.

TWIN Buckets there lived in a well.
This is their Parable.

Said the one, as he downward went,
With a rattle of discontent :

"What folly ! drawn full to the top,
Returning with never a drop !"

Quoth his mate, coming skyward, " Why, nay !
I see it another way.

" However thirsty we sink,
We rise with a plenty to drink !"

Life's tapestry's woven so that it
Shines just as you choose to look at it,

And responds, as your wisdom hath struck it,
Like a full or an empty bucket !

THE SPHINX.

THE Sphinx by the Desert stands,
Lord of the lonely lands,
With the dust of the Desert sands
On its head, and its heart, and its hands.

Ages before the Flood
Ere the Delta grew out of the mud,
Up to its knees it stood
In a deluge of tears and blood!

The Desert was out of sight
When the creature was dragged to light,
Out of the caves of Night,
And the Desert was puzzled quite.

'Twas a riddle they used to tell
At the digging of Joseph's well,
Ere the scourge of the Pharaohs fell
On the shoulders of Israel!

And there's never a star that winks
On Africa as it sinks
But wonders whenever it thinks
Of the world and its wonderful Sphinx.

And there's nothing by land or sea
Can ever expect to be
Such an ugly old puzzle as he
Except old Tyranny.

A riddle to rest unread
'Till the Pharaohs are *dead*,
Till the people shall toil for bread,
And not for a *stone* instead.

THE FARMER MAN.

TO W. N. N.

FYTTE I.

THE farmer man! I see him sit
In his low porch, to muse a bit
The while I throw him in a—Fytte.

What time the jasmines scent the air,
And drop their blossoms in his hair;

What time the evening echo tells
Of trampling herds and tinkling bells;

And all the echoes of the Ark
Salute the planter-patriarch!

So sitting with his collar spread,
And heels y'levelled with his head;

A monarch in his mere content,
A king by general consent.

FYTTE II.

And framed between his heels he sees
A picture, which perchance may please :

The distant city, and more nigh
The river's twinkle, like an eye

Obscured at intervals by motes,
Which quite extract its *beam* with *boats*.

The purple hills where, swift or slow,
The cloudless shadows come and go ;

While, dun as dormice, at their hem
The little cars follow them,

With all the clatter that portends
The most prodigious dividends !

The cottages with curling smoke,
Significant of "colored folk,"

The first without a foe or care,
To breathe Millennium's morning air,

And in their midst *a lovely mound
Most eloquent, without a sound,*

*Tells how the parting years have sped
With the black savage and the red.*

The yellow cornfields and the brown,
Where Southern snows have melted down,

And borne its all-abundant lint
To drown the mills and drain the mint.

The woods whose autumn glories cheer
The solemn sunset of the year,

With oval openings, which enshrine
Such views as we are picturing,

And hint how much the traveller sees
Who stays at home and studies trees,

And thanks the telescope, tho' dim,
That keeps its *smallest eye* on him,

And nearer home all shape and sheen
Of Nature's endless evergreen,

Through which a winding walk doth glide
To orchards, jubilant and wide,

Restrained within an emerald edge,
Of fair, tho' somewhat thorny hedge.

An archway entrance, and o'erhead
This little legend to be read :

" Partake of *all* the fruit, nor grieve
For Eden's morn or Eden's Eve !''

FYTTE III.

But what of him, the farmer man,
His way of life and being's plan?

Why simply (be it so with many!)
That "Now's as good a time as any."

Yet he can tell you of a morn
Ere yonder valley sang with corn,

Or yonder hill-top bared its brow,
Submissive to the sun and plow.

And long before yon proud white spires
Crushed out the low red council-fires.

With not a "turn-out" toe to press
The dim walks of the wilderness.

Of many a season come and flown,
With strokes of fortune and his own;

Till waves of varied memory
Shall leave him stranded as we see;

With time's old foam-marks in the lines,
Now starry with the jessamines.

FYTTE IV.

His politics I might rehearse
In limits lesser than my verse.

Should any tool my State invade,
Then mention *me* as strict "State aid."

Till then I mind my own affairs,
And trust my friends to manage theirs.

His science? such as thou may'st hit
By ploughing deep in search of it.

His wit? the shortest link that girds
An English thought to English words.

His credit? shall the world forget
The Atlas that upheld her debt?

His creed? in reverence of the past
Old faith and feeling holds he fast.

So that my muse's stenograph
Anticipates his epitaph,—

" He read the Bible, loved his wife,
And hated humbug all his life."

And, happily, to round my " pome,"
" Loved God, his neighbor, and his home."

MEMORIAL AND RELIGIOUS POEMS.

IN MEMORIAM.

THOMAS MADUIT NELSON, ÆTAT 71.

THEY fail from council and from camp, they are falling
    one by one,
Those grand old heroes of the stamp of God-loved
    Washington ;
The task is wrought of mighty minds, their glorious
    day is done,
And Freedom mourns a faded star with every setting
    sun.

The massive brow, the kindly hand, the proud and
    stalwart form
That stood as beacons in the night, as bulwarks in the
    storm.
Ah ! few and far on Glory's slope their lessening num-
    bers stand,
" The Pillars of a People's hope," the Titans of the
    land.

The mould is broken ; here no more those regal souls
    we meet
Who kept their honor, tho' the world had rocked be-
    neath their feet ;

The calm, clear dignity that shone no clearer for re-
 nown,
The matchless majesty that *won*, but would not *wear* a
 crown.

Ah! when descends the sullen night of Freedom's
 darkest hour,
When Demagogue and Parasite defile the seats of
 power,
When dust is on the eagle's crest, and stain on stripe
 and star,
Ah! who shall fill *their* robes in peace, or lift *their*
 swords in war?

One more to that immortal band, that long illustrious
 line,
That counts no nobler name, old friend, or purer soul
 than thine;
Yea, with the mighty in their death, their rest, and
 their reward,
Sleep, in thy cloudless Fame and *Faith*, true soldier of
 the Lord.

Sleep with the mighty in thy death! yet not with these
 alone;
Sleep with the loving hearts that beat so truly to thine
 own.
Sleep with the sword-cross on thy breast, the well-worn
 scabbard by,
Fit symbols of a soldier's rest and his reward on high.

WILLIAM NELSON CARTER.

SOLDIER OF THE SOUTH AT 16, OF THE CROSS AT 19,
DIED AT KEY WEST, AGED 21.

SPOKE from the stainless azure
   Of immemorial veins,
" War for the right is over,
   Battle for bread remains."

And he carried his bright smile from us,
   Our choral of bird and breeze,
To the light of the tideless summers,
   The song of the tropic seas.

So far !—yet his soul's clear brightness
   Drew nearer, and never cold ;
Found speech in the sea-bloom's whiteness,
   And kisses in fruits of gold.

And sweeter than day-spring's murmur
   To the palm when the spice-wind stirs
Were the voices that sang from the summer,—
   " Your darling has won his spurs !"

And we sang to the voice of the summer,
   With a smile that was glad to tears,—
" If your sea or your sand yield honor,
   Trust to the cavaliers !"

Sang !—with the summer stooping
　To shatter us, root and crest ;
With the lightning to signal "drooping,"
　And the thunder to crash " at rest."

Dumb ! and the clouds close o'er us,
　And the world reels blank and dim.
Blind ! with our hands before us
　Beseeching the mists for him.

Christ's soldier !   Through all the shadows
　One lily of light shall rise—
Not far ! though it smiles from the meadows
　And summers of Paradise.

MARY.

(MARY H. DILLINGHAM.)

SHALL I whisper a name that was lovely of old,
When the tale of the infant Redeemer was told,
The honored of God, in her sorrow sublime,
Still haunting the heart in the shadows of Time?

O'er the starlight of Judah the night mists were rolled ;
On the Galilee's bosom the shadows lay cold ;
When it woke on the midnight so solemn and dim,
With the flame of a star and the sound of a hymn,

And bright with the lustre and sweet with the tone
Of the angels that sang and the glory that shone.

Its echoes are soft, through the haze of the years,
With the breath of her sigh and the dew of her tears.

And still at the altar, and still at the hearth,
From the cradle of Christ to the ends of the earth,
As gentle in glory, as steadfast in gloom,
It serves at His side, as it knelt at His tomb.

And many shall bless it, and many have blest,
From the morning of life till the morrow of rest;
And its fulness of meaning its music shall keep
While a Mary shall watch or a Mary shall weep.

THE CHURCHYARD CROSS.

So, clasp thine arms about the Cross,
  And bow thy little head;
Draw close the only links between
  Our sorrows and our dead.

So, fold thy pinions round the Cross,
  Sweet dove, and feel no fear;
No note but one of tenderness
  Shall ever meet thee here.

And from the mound of sacred earth
  Our sundered hearts between,
Draw thou the fragrance of her worth,
  To keep her memory green.

LITTLE KATIE.

The Lily we love! it is whiter
  For the darkness that covers the day;
The pearl of our souls! it is brighter
  For the shadows that turn to gray.

To the sunlight that calls, its tender,
  Pale petals are closed and chill;
To the dew, though it falls from the splendor
  Of stars, it is silent still.

Let the darkness fall *deep*, and deliver
  Unveiled to our weary eyes
The pearl by the Eden River—
  Our Lily in Paradise.

OUR TREASURE IN HEAVEN.

Sleep sweetly, gentle one;
  Sleep till thy shrouded eyes
Shall waken 'mid the Bowers of God,
  Oh, Bird of Paradise!

Oh, softest, gentlest hands
  Did soothe thee to thy rest;
And the pure souls that welcomed thee
  Were highest of the blest.

Often we'll call thy name,
   And the pure joy it brings
Shall cheer us as the rustling sound
   Of thy young seraph's wings.

The hosts that follow thee
   To the pure Throne of God
Shall find no shadow in the vale
   Thy little feet have trod.

"THE CHILDREN THAT ARE NOT."

THE children—the children that are not! Ah, why
From the ends of the earth swells that desolate cry?
Has the dull earth a glory, the bright skies a gloom,
That a wail should arise at the gates of the tomb?

Ah! deem ye the sparrow its pathway may hold,
Yet a lamb of Christ's love be lost from his fold?
That the diamond's sparkle should never burn dim,
Yet a spirit be quenched that was kindled by Him?

Are the husbandman's tears with his toil in vain?
From the scattered seed shall there spring no grain?
Hath the chrysalis wings ere its shroud is wound?
Hath the violet breath in the dull cold ground?

Yea! bless ye God, as ye bend above
The broken lilies of tears and love,
That not without witness the hope was given
That a "little child" should be first in Heaven.

Yea ! bear them to rest 'mid the flowers that tell
Their Master's meaning so clear and well,
And know by their pathway an angel hath trod
From the brightness of earth to the bosom of God !

FAITH.

WHY sits pale Sorrow at the gate of Heaven,
　With eyes so wan, such wild and haggard air,
As one whose woe with God's own arm had striven,
　And won the triumph of a wild despair ?

Crouched where the shadow of the marble portal
　Falls deep and deeper on her clouded eyes,
Speeding with wail and cry the feet immortal
　That enter there the walks of Paradise !

Angel of Faith ! shall sullen sorrow render
　Thy smile a *mockery* to the hearts that mourn ?
Deepen the gloom, yet not reveal the splendor
　Where *Saints* depart and *Seraphim* are born ?

Star of our hearts ! what other light may linger,
　When on our eyes the tomb's black shadow falls,
If thou trace not with thine uplifted finger
　The gathering glory on its inner walls ?

And thou ! on thine own gentle bosom blending
　The broken lilies of our tears and love,
Lighten the pathway where our feet are tending,
　Lengthen the cords that guide our hearts above !

SONG BY NIGHT.

And are these the days of the darkening haze,
 The mists whence no star may quiver?
And is this the moan of the monotone
 Of the dark and tideless river?
We look not back on our weary track
 For the voice of a vanished chorus;
The lights are gone that have led us on,
 But the path lies straight before us.

Let the hair grow white, let the failing sight
 Await but a clouded morrow;
We keep the faith that we pledged to death
 And the troth we plighted sorrow!
There are flowers that bloom by the quiet tomb
 Of the gentle, the true, and tender;
And they are all that our prayers recall,
 Or the sepulchre can surrender!

Are there forms as fair as we buried there?
 Are there lips with such fragrance laden?
Are there sounds as sweet as the bounding feet
 That are white 'mid the lilies of Aidenne?
It may be so, but they bring no glow
 To hearts that are haunted ever
By the shadow that lies on the shrouded eyes,
 And the lips that are sealed forever.

Bid Death remove from the brows we love
    The damps of his dark'ning river;
Let Heaven restore on its shining shore
    The lost whom we love forever!
Their light alone on our pathway thrown,
    Their star to our darkness given,
Shall lend its fires to the trembling wires
    That are linked to our hearts and Heaven.

TO MRS. L. E. C.

UPBORNE by angels in a world of sorrow,
    In others' anguish losing half her own;
So taught of grief that darkened souls might borrow
    Their light of sunshine from her lips alone!

Herself a seraph, whose unfolding pinions
    And upward glance betray her better birth,
Yet lingering still amid the dull world's minions
    To win some wanderer from the ills of earth.

As fair of form as lily-pure of spirit,
    Heaven watched, yet humble in her upward way;
Ah! such as *she* are they who shall inherit
    The strength and triumph of a better day.

LINES.

You may call: she will come! Not the shadow of
    night
  Shrouds a sorrow she shuns to meet,
And you shall not know by her step so light
  That sharpness hath pierced her feet:

That the balm of her healing was bruised of pain,
  The breath of a smitten lyre;
That the touch, so cool to your fevered brain,
  Was purified by fire.

But you shall believe that a wing so swift,
  And a voice of so sweet a tone,
Shall shine with the stars when the clouds uplift,
  And sing by the great white Throne.

ILLUMINATING LETTERS.

SHE wrought: and at her reverent touch,
That lingered long in loving much,

As to the sunlight and the dew
The tendril twined, the floweret grew,

Till burned around each holy name
A brightness as of altar flame;

Anthem and incense in each word
That bore the blossom or the bird;

Each letter's self a shrine, where *art*
Uttered the worship of the heart.

And still she wrought; and still her touch,
That lingered long in loving much,

Recalled *their* task in that old time
Who saw the slow cathedral climb,

Grand with the prayers of many days,
And glowing in its orb of praise;

Unfolding, as it neared the skies,
A Passion-flower of centuries;

Rich in all grace that love alone
Can learn of Heaven, or teach to stone;

Such love as waits the dawn, and gave
The watch at midnight to His grave,

Steadfast and tireless, till the hour
Unveils the Temple's perfect Flower,

"Christ!" May He wreathe, as these are wrought,
Our lives with grace of deed and thought!

THE CEMETERY.

A CHURCHYARD walk, and by the way
 We saw, on either hand,
More symbols of the world's "decay"
 Than of the "better land!"

With more of rigid carpentry,
 And less of bloom and leaf,
Than tokened brotherhood in death,
 Or fellowship in grief.

And yet, without these mouldering pales,
 'Twere easy to o'erspread,
With Eden grace, these silent vales,
 This city of the dead.

Without this mass of tangled brier
   Yon oak were not less green ;
And happily yon Heavenward spire
   Were *more* distinctly seen !

The "vexed Bermuda" here might rest
   In undisturbed retreat,
On many a long-forgotten breast
   And long-neglected street.

The dead white column, cross and urn
   With Olive shadowed o'er,
Might teach us, when we come to mourn,
   This much, if nothing more :

That vainly o'er our lost delights
   The pomp of marble towers,
Without the gentle care that writes
   Its Martha-thought in flowers.

THE BEAUTY OF HOLINESS.

RECALL—while now thy longing gaze,
Grows dim with more than autumn's haze—
Of all the walks thy feet have pressed,
That path the *peacefullest* to *rest :*

Of fountains that thy need have nursed,
That "well" the *sweetest* to thy thirst :

Of flowers—and lo ! thy hands were full—
That blossom *the most beautiful :*

Of touch and tone, through all the past,
The *tenderest* and lingering last :

That radiance of the vanished years,
Most radiant for thy very tears.

Name that which, trembling like a star,
Shines with our loved and lost, so far ;

Yet nearest to our inner dreams
Brings the soft flow of Eden's streams ;

Lighting the shadow where we stand
With angel eyes on either hand.

Mute lips, or with hosannas, these
Bear witness with our memories,

In music blending to express
Pure beauty in its perfectness—
Earth's charm, Heaven's glory—
" Holiness."

EASTER.

CHRIST ! *arisen ?*   Lift your eyes !
Lo ! what glory fills the skies !
Winter's death is dead, and born
The summer's hope in springing corn.
While the lily cleaves the sod,
Who shall bind the Son of God?

Christ ! *arise ?*   The sun to-day
Unseals a tomb, and rolls away
All mists of midnight like a stone ;
All raiment save of light alone.
Shall the single shadow fall
On the Christ, the Lord of all?

Christ ! *arisen ?*   Roman steel
Sentineled that stone and seal.
Rome, in her imperial power,
Watched until the dawning hour,—
Watched and *witnessed !* bowed and said,
" Christ is risen from the dead !"

Oh, by all an Age's trust !
By our darlings laid in dust !

In our griefs the single stay ;
Of our joys the central ray ;
Cease, my Doubt, thy sentry tread !
" Christ is risen from the dead ! "

THE CHURCH.

DEAR Mother ! in this weary waste
    And wilderness of woe,
How sweet the smile, how soft the rest
    Thy little children know !

The trumpet's clangor at thy wall
    Stirs not thy peace above ;
We hear, and only hear, the call
    Of our dear Mother's love.

Her touch upon our infant brow,
    Her tears above our dead,
Her tones of tenderness, are now
    As in the years that fled.

Nor fades of all her bloom and balm
    One blossom from her wreath,
More radiant in celestial calm
    For all the storms beneath.

Bright Beacon ! nearest to the skies
    Of all that light the sea.
Blest Haven ! where our treasure lies,
    And where our hearts would be.

Most steadfast as our pillars fall
  And pride and pleasures cease.
Earth's sorrows! who hath known them all,
  Best knows thy perfect peace.

THE END.

www.ingramcontent.com/pod-product-compliance
Lightning Source LLC
Chambersburg PA
CBHW020235030726
47497CB00009B/3099